What is a girl?
What is a boy?
by Stephanie Waxman

Thomas Y. Crowell   New York

Photo Credits
David by Robert Liu
Jessica by Dennis Hicks
All others by Stephanie Waxman

For their enthusiastic support, my heartfelt thanks to
Dennis Hicks
Alice Simmons
Barbara Black
Richard Prieffer

And to all the people who let me use their pictures
in this book.

What is a girl? What is a boy?
Copyright © 1976, 1989 by Stephanie Waxman
First published by Peace Press, Culver City, California
Typography by Cathryn S. Aison

Library of Congress Cataloging-in-Publication Data
Waxman, Stephanie, 1944–
    What is a girl? what is a boy? / by Stephanie Waxman.
        p.   cm.
    Summary: Simple text and photographs explain the biological
differences between males and females and illustrate the
similarities between the sexes.
    ISBN 0-690-04709-6 : $.   ISBN 0-690-04711-8 (lib. bdg.) : $
    1. Sex instruction for children.   2. Sex role in children—
Juvenile literature.   3. Sex differences—Juvenile literature.
[1. Sex instruction for children.   2. Sex role.   3. Sex differences.]   I. Title.
HQ53.W39   1989   87-36528
612.6′007—dc19   CIP
                                                        AC

10   9   8   7   6   5   4   3   2   1
New Edition

For my children
Jessica
Tessa

Foreword

A mother was standing in line at the bank with her three-year-old daughter. The child was staring intently at the teller, a young man in his early twenties. Finally it was the mother's turn. She sat the child on the narrow counter and opened her checkbook. Suddenly the little girl asked the teller in a loud voice, "Do you have a penis?" The young man blushed. The people around them tittered. "I'm sorry," muttered the woman, as she quickly lowered the little girl to the floor. "She's just a child."

It's true. The little girl was acting just like a child. Young children are little scientists, and like other children her age, she was doing what any good scientist would do: collecting evidence to support her hypothesis: "All men have penises."

All young children go through periods of uncertainty about issues relating to sexuality. In an effort to sort through their confusion, children often divide along sex lines with a passion: "Only girls can play in the playhouse!" "Only boys can be Superman!" "Boys are ugly!" "Girls are dumb!" The need to separate themselves by sex is part of the struggle to discover their sexual identities.

Enlightened adults are apt to play down the differences between the sexes and encourage the similarities in an effort to foster equality and nonsexist attitudes. Yet in doing so, we may be disregarding the child's need for elementary information. Often children don't know the simple biological differences between being a girl and being a boy (or a woman and a man), even though they realize they are one or the other. No wonder they gravitate toward the sexist models our society offers in their efforts to understand who they are.

This book may make some children giggle and titter at first. It may make some adults uncomfortable, too. Most of us get nervous discussing issues pertaining to sexuality with anyone, let alone with a child. Yet because this book provides information in a nonthreatening way, it can diffuse the embarrassment that surrounds discussions of sexuality and, by reassuring, make children comfortable with themselves and with the opposite sex.

Stephanie Waxman
Venice, California

What is a girl?
What is a boy?

A baby is either a girl
or a boy.

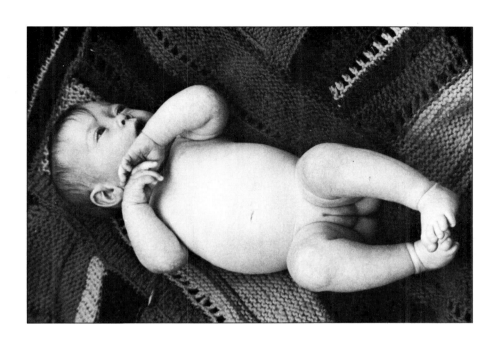

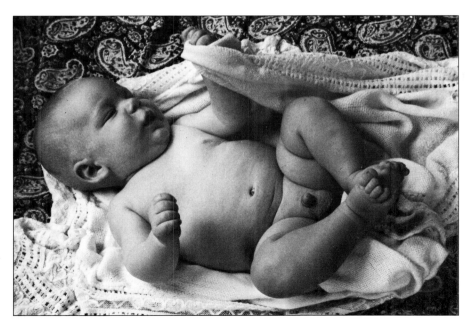

If the baby is a girl,
she will always be a girl.

Jessica used to be a baby girl.
Now she is a three-year-old girl.

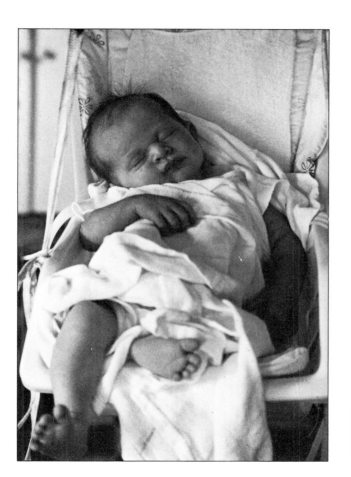

If the baby is a boy,
he will always be a boy.

David used to be a baby boy.
Now he is a four-year-old boy.

What is a girl?
Some people say a girl
is someone with long hair.

But Chung has long hair.
And he's a boy.

What is a boy?
Some people say a boy
is someone with short hair.

But Mimi has short hair.
And she's a girl.

Some people say a girl
is someone with jewelry.

But Derrick is wearing a bracelet.
And he's a boy.

Some people say a boy
is someone wearing pants.

But Keko is wearing pants.
And she's a girl.

Some people say a girl
is someone with a girl's name.

Sam is usually a boy's name.
But this Sam is a girl.

Some people say a boy
is someone who plays basketball.

But Rosa is playing basketball.
And she's a girl.

Some people say a girl
is someone who plays with dolls.

But Noah is taking care of his doll.
And he's a boy.

Some people say a boy
is someone who is strong.

But Lola is lifting a heavy block.
And she's a girl.

Some people say a boy
is someone who doesn't cry.

But Eric is crying.
And he's a boy.

Then what *is* a boy?

A boy is someone
with a penis and testicles.

Every boy has a penis and testicles.

And what *is* a girl?

A girl is someone
with a vulva and a vagina.

Every girl has a vulva and a vagina.

If you are a boy,
you will grow up to be a man.
Every man has a penis and testicles.

When Gary became a man,
his voice got deeper,
and hair grew on parts of his body.

If you are a girl,
you will grow up to be a woman.
Every woman has a vulva and a vagina.

When Natalie became a woman,
her breasts got bigger,
and hair grew on parts of her body.

Are you a girl or are you a boy?